This book belongs to:

A Bug-a-Boo Day Play

A Bug-a-Boo Day Play

CALLAWAY
NEW YORK
2008

Miss Spider's children were putting on a play to celebrate Bug-a-Boo Day, the spookiest day of the year. Miss Spider was sewing bug costumes for their show.

"A play is a lot of work, kids,"
Miss Spider reminded them.

"But if everyone helps,"
Shimmer replied,
"it will be fun, too!"

The next morning, the kids began building a stage.

Snack the Ladybug came by. "Will you come to my pumpkin party tonight?"

"Sure, Snack," Shimmer replied. "After our play."

"I'll help pick pumpkins for the party!" Dragon exclaimed, and flew away.

"We should probably help Dragon," Pansy said, as she and Wiggle followed him.

"Okay, but hurry back," Shimmer called. "We still have a lot of work to do."

Spinner kept working on the stage, but he was tired.

"Shimmer . . . this . . . is . . . taking . . . longer . . . than I . . . thought," he panted. "I need to take a b-b-b-reak!"

Just then, Beetrice Bee buzzed by.

"Anybuggy want to taste my Bug-a-Boo treats?" she called.

"ME! ME! ME!" Bounce yelled, hurrying off, with Squirt and Snowdrop right behind him.

Shimmer was sad that her brothers and sisters had left. "This play is more work than I thought it would be."

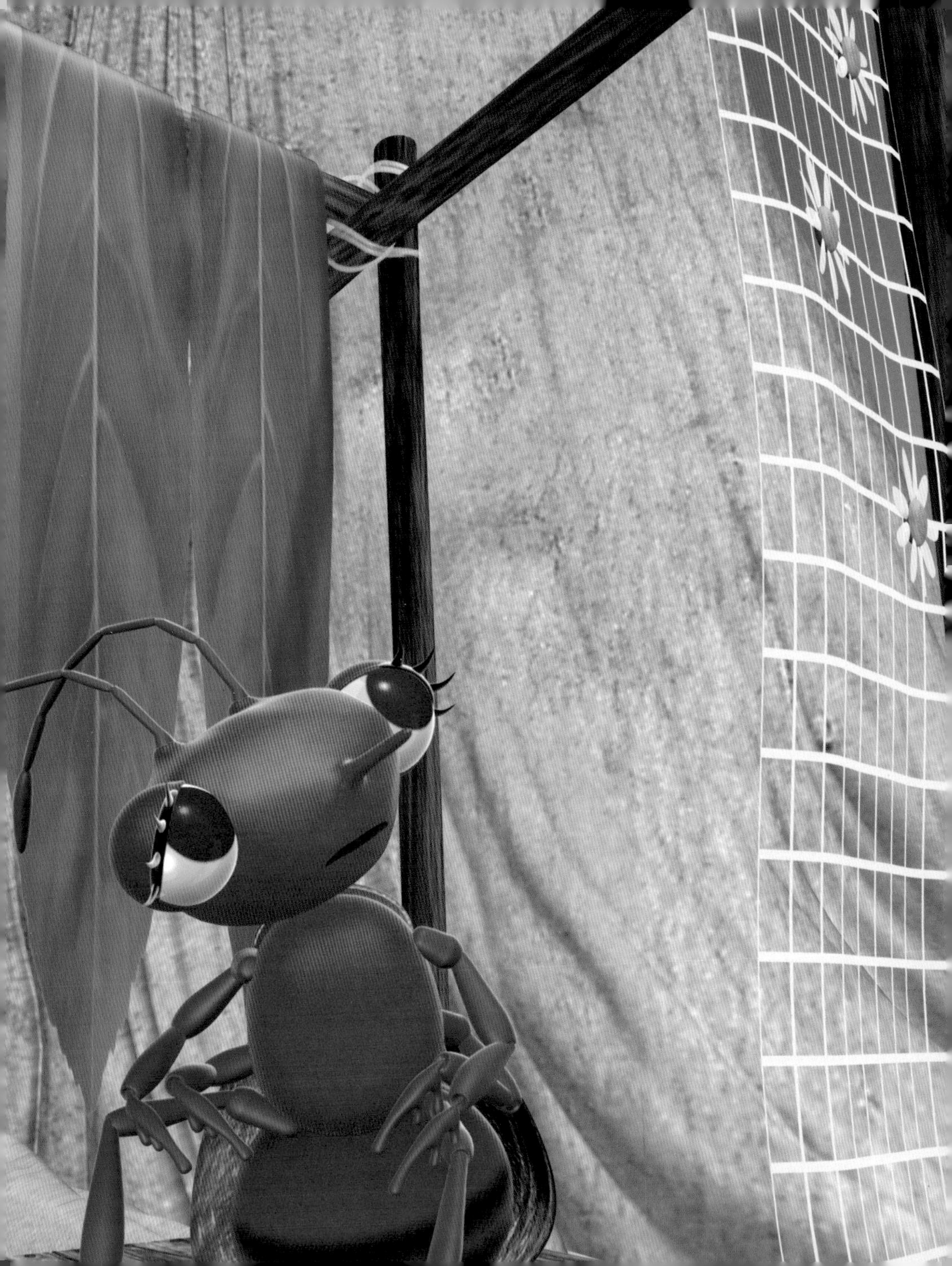

When Miss Spider and Holley arrived, they were surprised to see Shimmer alone on the stage.

"My Bug-a-Boo Day play turned out to be a Bug-a-Boo Day boo-boo," Shimmer cried.

"But you've still got the stage, the sets, and even the costumes," Miss Spider told her. "With a little imagination, you can have your play after all."

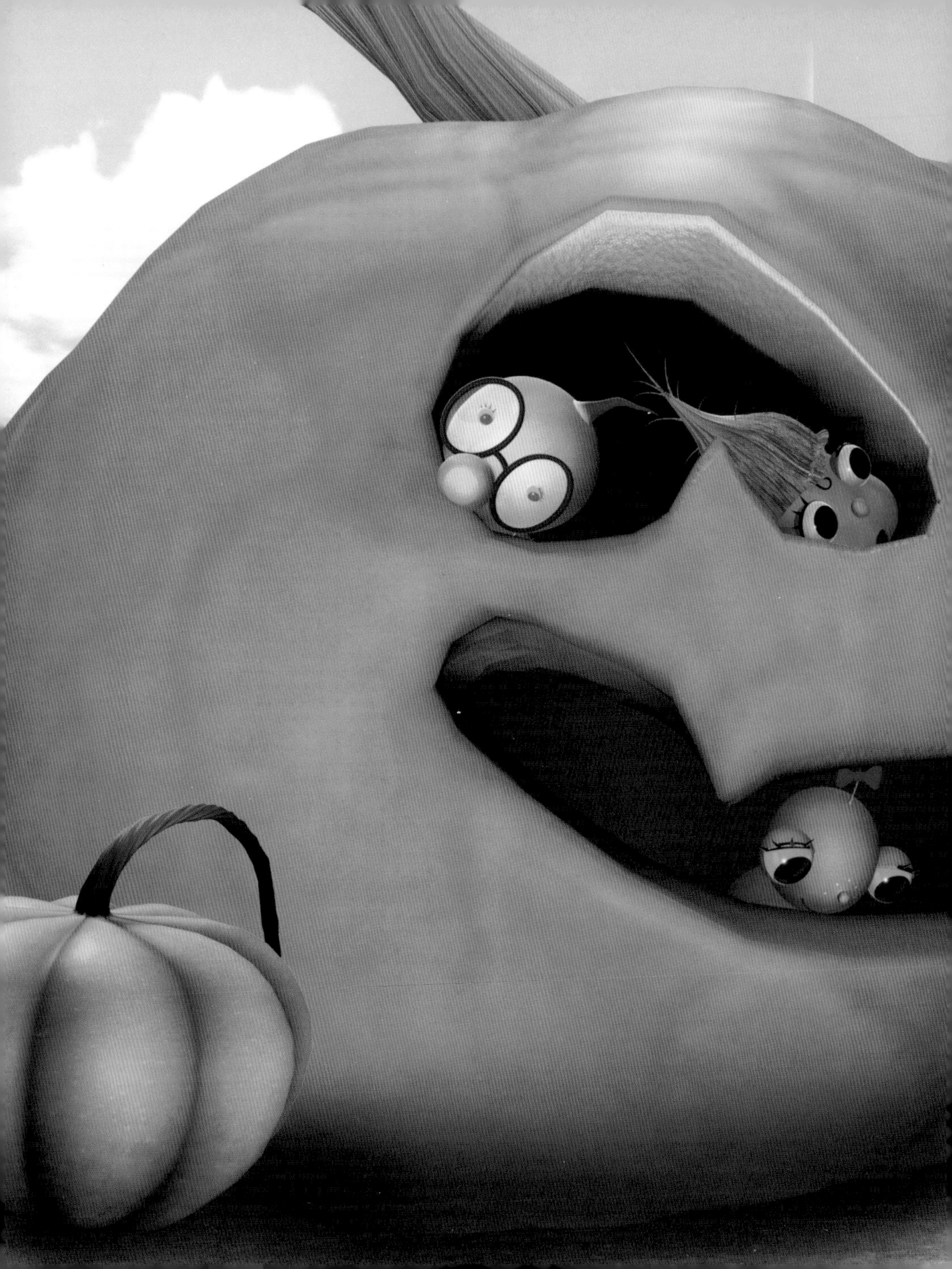

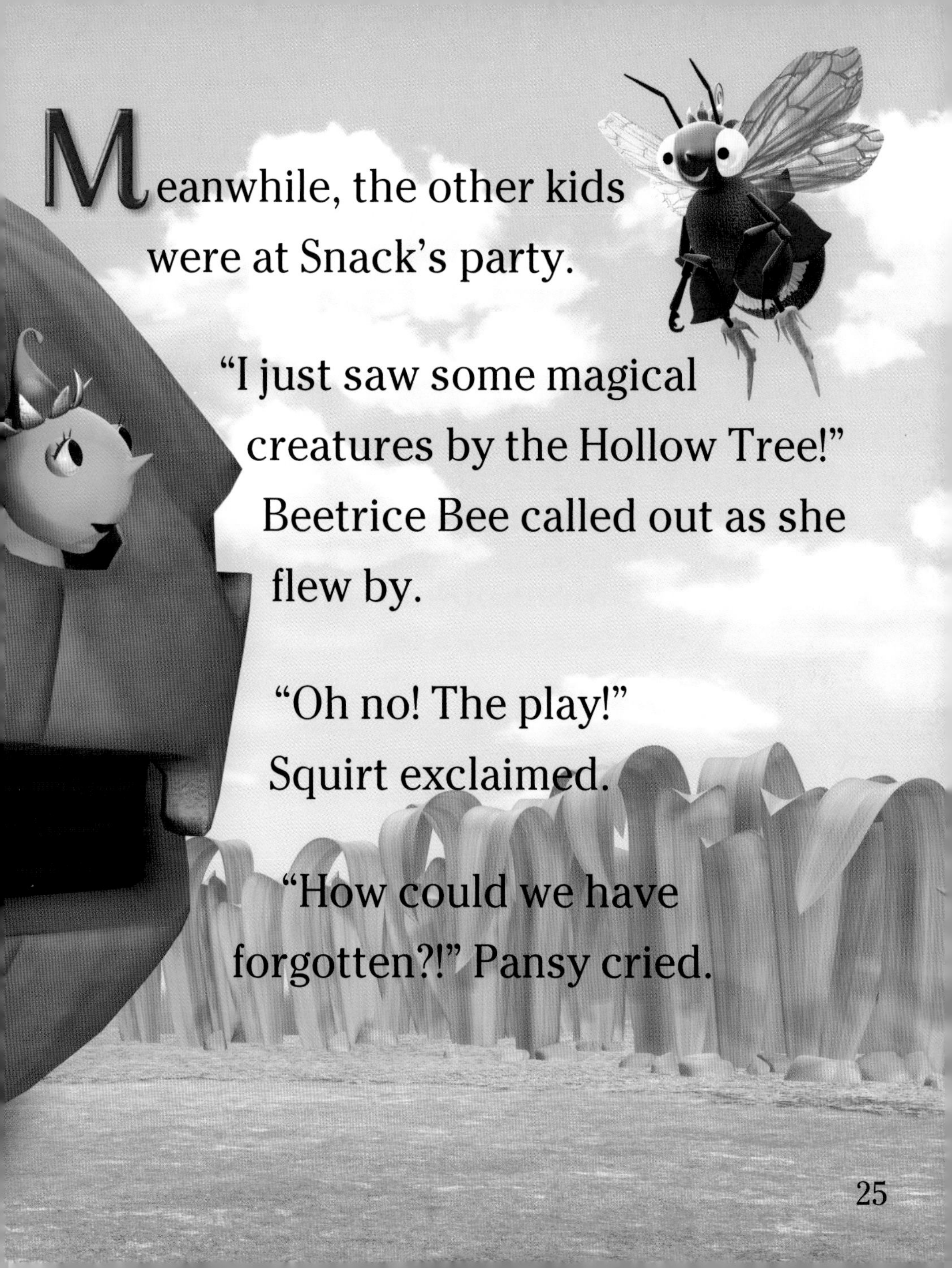

Meanwhile, the other kids were at Snack's party.

"I just saw some magical creatures by the Hollow Tree!" Beetrice Bee called out as she flew by.

"Oh no! The play!" Squirt exclaimed.

"How could we have forgotten?!" Pansy cried.

On stage, everyone's costumes seemed to be dancing back and forth in mid-air while Shimmer sang a song.

"Wow," Dragon said. "How did Shimmer get them to move?"

"Looks like Mom pulled a few strings," Squirt said, pointing upward.

"Your show's a huge hit, honey," Miss Spider said as everyone clapped.

"We're sorry we let you down, Shimmer," Squirt said.

"It was a spiderific show," added Dragon.

"That's okay, guys,"
Shimmer replied.
"HAPPY BUG-A-BOO DAY!"

This book is based on the TV episode "A Bug-a-Boo Day Play," written by Steven Sullivan, from the animated TV series *Miss Spider's Sunny Patch Friends* on Nick Jr., a Nelvana Limited/Absolute Pictures Limited co-production in association with Callaway Arts & Entertainment, based on the Miss Spider books by David Kirk.

Published by Grosset & Dunlap, a division of Penguin Young Readers Group, 345 Hudson Street, New York, New York 10014, in association with Callaway Arts & Entertainment.
GROSSET & DUNLAP is a trademark of Penguin Group (USA) Inc.
Printed in China. Digital Art by Callaway Animation Studio under the direction of David Kirk in collaboration with Nelvana Limited.

ISBN 978-0-448-45024-7 10 9 8 7 6 5 4 3 2 1

ABOUT DAVID KIRK

Master artist and storyteller David Kirk is hailed as one of today's most innovative and exciting creators of books and toys for children. Before his remarkable success in the world of children's publishing, Kirk was the founder and designer of two toy companies. His bright, hand-painted wooden toys are, together with his paintings and hand-crafted furniture, treasured by collectors and featured in books, art galleries, and museums.

Then along came a spider: Miss Spider. Inspired by his daughter Violet's love for insects in the family garden, Kirk found the perfect subject for his story. *Miss Spider's Tea Party,* a lush counting book in verse with mesmerizing oil illustrations and an important message about tolerance, quickly became a phenomenon, earning praise from booksellers and librarians across the country. Kirk followed this success by continuing the saga of Miss Spider in *Miss Spider's Wedding, Miss Spider's New Car,* and *Miss Spider's ABC.*

In addition to creating splendid books and paintings, Mr. Kirk finds time to develop his many other projects, including designing Sunny Patch, a collection of children's lifestyle products, for Target stores. He is also executive producer of *Miss Spider's Sunny Patch Friends,* a 3-D computer-animated television series on Nick Jr. The success of the series inspired a line of trade and mass-market books published by Callaway Arts & Entertainment and Penguin Young Readers Group.

Mr. Kirk lives in upstate New York with his wife, Kathy, and daughters, Violet, Primrose, and Wisteria.